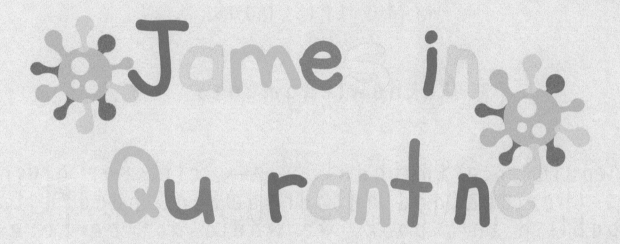

James in Quarantine

Written by Julie Adair and Kaitlyn Boddez

This book is dedicated to our teacher Mrs. Hall, who has been there for us through our journey as musicians and now writers. Mrs. Hall and her love for teaching is the whole reason we decided to write this book.

Acknowledgments

We would like to thank Mrs. Zelt, for giving us the idea and encouragement needed to publish this book, we would not be here without her and all that she has done for us.

We would also like to thank our parents for believing in us through this whole process and really being the ones who made this possible.

On a sunny afternoon, James wanted to go outside and play with his friends. But James wasn't allowed. James was having a tough time with the new isolation rules, because of the new sickness outside.

Even though James couldn't go outside, he realized he could still have fun inside. James ran down the stairs, grabbed his little sister Ava, and they started planning for their first quarantine adventure.

They decided to build a rocket ship! They ran to the garage and grabbed all the supplies needed to build a super cool, brand-new rocket ship.

Their rocket ship was complete and they started on their space adventure!

"I want to fly the ship" says James. "Fine. I'll be the astronaut princess" yelled Ava.

After they had played in their rocket ship for a while, James realized they needed to find their next adventure inside the house. James didn't have an idea yet, so he asked Ava.

"What should we do Ava?"

"Let's go swimming!" she replied.

"We can't go swimming, remember?"

"I have an idea, but we will need a lot of colorful paper" said James

"What are we going to do with all this paper" Ava asked James.

"We are going to make an underwater adventure Ava" James so proudly announced.

And so they started cutting out fish, and James started filling the bathtub and they began their underwater adventure.

"Let's dive in!" said James as the bathtub transformed into an underwater world.

"How did you do that James?"

"With your imagination Ava".

"I'm tired of swimming James, let's go do something else."
Ava said after a wonderful time in the bathtub.

"Okay Ava", replied James so they get dressed and
started looking around for what they could do next.

Ava saw Mom and Dad upstairs on the couch. "They look tired James" Ava observed. James saw Mom and Dad and that they were sleeping. James had to think. This was going to be the biggest surprise ever!

James thought of an idea, he whispered it to Ava, and they started to work.

Ava grabbed her colors, as James ran to the kitchen. James started making his masterpiece and Ava started decorating.

"Mom, Dad!" James yelled when they were done their last adventure. "Open your eyes" said Ava, excited to see their reactions.

Mom and Dad both woke up to see that James and Ava made a BIG surprise.

Mom and Dad were speechless. Ava had decorated their entire living room with colored stars on the walls, and James had made them both supper - Peanut Butter and Jam Sandwiches!

"Thanks guys!" said Dad. "I love you both so much" said Mom. And they both bit into their delicious sandwiches for dinner.

Even though this is a different experience, us all being stuck inside right now, we all have each other. We can make our own adventures and still have a lot of fun, even when we are inside. The most important thing to do, is to stay safe!

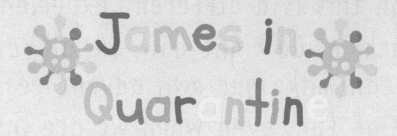

James in Quarantine

Follow James and his younger sister Ava through their journey around their house, finding masterpieces to create, new worlds to live in, and adventures to go on. "James in Quarantine" shows kids of all ages that there are lots of fun things to do while stuck inside and how to have a better attitude about it all!